STELLA

PRINCESS OF THE SKY

MARIE-LOUISE GAY

GROUNDWOOD BOOKS
HOUSE OF ANANSI PRESS
TORONTO   BERKELEY

Groundwood Books / House of Anansi Press
110 Spadina Avenue, Suite 801, Toronto, Ontario M5V 2K4
Distributed in the USA by Publishers Group West
1700 Fourth Street, Berkeley, CA 94710

We acknowledge for their financial support of our publishing program the Canada
Council of the Arts, the Government of Canada through the Canada Book Fund
(CBF) and the Ontario Arts Council.

Canada Council   Conseil des Arts
for the Arts   du Canada

ONTARIO ARTS COUNCIL
CONSEIL DES ARTS DE L'ONTARIO

Library and Archives Canada Cataloguing
in Publication
Gay, Marie-Louise
Stella, princess of the sky / by Marie-Louise Gay
ISBN: 978-1-55498-072-7
I. Title.
PS8563.A868S729 2010   jC813'.54   C2010-902460-5

The illustrations were done in watercolor, HB pencil, pastel, collage of
handmade Japanese paper and touches of acrylic paint.

Printed and bound in China

For Alain l'oursin

"Stella!" cried Sam. "Stella! Look!
The sky is on fire!"

"No, it isn't, Sam," said Stella. "The sun is just going to sleep."
"Why is it so red?" asked Sam.
"Can't you see? It's wearing red pajamas."

"Pajamas?" said Sam. "Like mine?"
"Of course," said Stella, "and when the moon rises,
it wraps the sun up in a big starry blanket."

"Where does the sun sleep?" asked Sam. "On a bed?"
"On a fluffy cloud," said Stella. "And every morning,
the sun jumps into the sky…

Like this!"
"Except when it rains," said Sam.
"Yes," said Stella. "Then the sun sleeps in."

"I know! Let's camp outside tonight," said Stella.
"Outside?" said Sam. "Won't it be cold and dark?"

"We'll have blankets and a flashlight."
"Won't there be mosquitoes?" whispered Sam. "Or giant moths?"
"Come on, Sam!" called Stella.

"Listen!" cried Sam. "Was that a wolf?"
"Wolves don't croak, Sam. That was a tree frog."
"Is a tree frog as big as a wolf?" asked Sam.

"It's so tiny you can put it in your pocket."
"There's no room in my pocket," said Sam. "It's full of cookies."
"Tree frogs love cookies," said Stella.

"Here, this is perfect. We'll see the moon coming up over the lake."
"Does the moon live in the lake?" asked Sam. "Does it swim?"
"No, it lives in the sky," answered Stella, "with the stars."

"Can the moon fly, then? Does it have wings?"
"The moon floats in the air," said Stella, "like a balloon."
"Who's holding the string?" asked Sam.

"HOO! HOO! HOO!"
"Who's that?" whispered Sam.

"That's an owl," said Stella. "He wants to know who we are."
"I'm Sam," called Sam. "And she's Stella."

"Look how fast those bats can fly!" said Stella.
"Don't they get caught in your hair?" asked Sam.
"No, bats are afraid of people. They won't come near us."

"I'm not afraid of bats," said Sam. "Not at all."
"Are you going to catch one with your butterfly net?"
"Oh, no," said Sam. "I'm going to catch a shooting star."

"You'll have to be quick as lightning," said Stella.
"It'll be easy," said Sam. "The grass is full of stars."

"Those are fireflies," said Stella.
"They light the way for all the other bugs."

"Do they burn?" asked Sam.
"No, they tickle! Do you want to hold one, Sam?"

"I think I'd rather watch it fly," said Sam.

"Who turned off the moon?" cried Sam. "I can't see."
"There's a cloud in front of the moon, Sam."

"But, now look! A raccoon family!" whispered Stella.
"Why are they wearing masks?" asked Sam. "Are they robbers?"
"No, they're going to a costume party," said Stella.

"There must be a million stars!" cried Stella.
"That's the Big Dipper...and there's the Milky Way.
Isn't it beautiful, Sam?"

"It looks like the moon spilled a glass of milk," said Sam.
"A really big one."

"And that's the North Star...it tells you where the North Pole is."
"So if a polar bear gets lost, it can find its way?" asked Sam.
"Of course," said Stella, "if it follows that star."

"But what if I get lost?" asked Sam.
"You can follow me," said Stella.

"How come you know so much about the stars, Stella?"
"Last summer, Grandma told me all about them.
Now, whenever I see stars, I always think of her."

"I always think of Grandma when I smell flowers," said Sam.

"I miss her," added Sam.
"Let's go see her soon," said Stella.
"Yes," whispered Sam.